A ROSE FOR PINKERTON

Story and pictures by
STEVEN KELLOGG

Dial Books for Young Readers

New York

a pied piper book ®

Dial Books for Young Readers
2 Park Avenue
New York, New York 10016

Copyright © 1981 by Steven Kellogg
All rights reserved.
Library of Congress Catalog Card Number: 81-65848
First Pied Piper Printing 1984
Printed in Hong Kong by South China Printing Co.
COBE
10 9 8 7 6 5 4
A Pied Piper Book is a registered trademark of
Dial Books for Young Readers
® TM 1,163,686 and ® TM 1,054,312

A ROSE FOR PINKERTON
is published in a hardcover edition by
Dial Books for Young Readers.
ISBN 0-8037-0060-1

The process art consists of black line-drawings,
black halftones, and full-color washes. The black line
is prepared and photographed separately for greater
contrast and sharpness. The full-color washes and
the black halftones are prepared with ink, crayons,
and paints on the reverse side of the black line-drawing.
They are then camera-separated and reproduced as
red, blue, yellow, and black halftones.

And another for Helen

Pinkerton, are you lonely? Do you miss curling
up with your brothers and sisters?

We should get some other Great Dane puppies
to play with Pinkerton.

I think he's trying to tell you that he agrees with me.

One Great Dane is enough! The only other pet I would consider would be something small and quiet...like a goldfish.

I'll go find a friend for you, Pinkerton.

This is the perfect place!

Pinkerton couldn't curl up with a goldfish.

And he couldn't play with a bird.

Maybe a kitten would be just right!

It says here in my book that Great Dane puppies
and kittens can become good friends.

Here's a surprise for you and Pinkerton.
Her name is Rose.

It says in this book by Sarah Chattercat that Great
Dane puppies and kittens can become good friends.

He seems to like her.

Rose took over Pinkerton's sun spot.

She's eating his dinner.

I think Rose wants to be a Great Dane.

Oh, no!

Now Pinkerton is trying to be a kitten!

Let's go back to that pet show! I have a
few questions for Sarah Chattercat!

Rose! Come back!

Pinkerton will be safe with the kittens.
Help me find Rose.

Rose! Where are you?

I see her! She's in line for the Grand March of the Poodles!

I'd like to welcome our television audience to this stunning event and to introduce Dr. Aleasha Kibble of Canine University, who will present the Golden Poodle Trophy.

Stop the ceremony! Call the police! The Grand March has been infiltrated by a feline impostor!

Excuse us, but that's our cat, Rose. She used to think she was a Great Dane but she's decided to be a poodle.

Ladies and gentlemen, the crowd and the poodles have gone berserk!

They are chasing the intruding cat toward the Castle of the Kittens!

There's a monster in the Castle of the Kittens.

Arrest that brute! He terrified our poodles,
and they've all fainted!

Nonsense! This wonderful dog saved the kittens.
He's a hero!

Does she still think she's a poodle?
Or is she a Great Dane again?

She's purring!